The Colour Of Water

A book of eclectic short stories, flash fiction and microfiction

Arunima Hoskote

Ukiyoto Publishing

Dedication

I dedicate this book to my father, Capt. Anil Hoskote, my inspiration to forge ahead always, and that motivation is reflected in each of my characters in this book.

Foreword

Arunima Hoskote is one of my fellow writers in the City Lit Strays writing group, the continuation of a short story writing course that started on zoom during the Covid pandemic lockdown of 2020. We are all in the UK except Arunima who lives in India and brings a different and welcoming perspective.

Arunima's short stories, flash and micro fiction cover a wide range of human predicaments. The Colour of Water, A New Dawn and Walking with Ghosts are inspired by real historical events; Poppies is a vivid snapshot of the ongoing Ukraine War, perhaps any war. Noor is set in India; others are in various locations, including a rehabilitation centre for suicidal patients (And Winter Came) and the hereafter (On the Other Side of the Comfort Zone). The Dark Room is a universal tale of revenge and retribution. The stories share a raw emotional appeal.

We started out on a short story writing course, but as a writing group with time and work constraints, we put this form on hold and embraced flash fiction, which is enjoying a twenty-first-century moment. We discovered that a line-up of unrelated words from an internet word generator can unlock ideas for stories that shoot off in surprising and rewarding directions.

Some of Arunima's flash and micro fiction is the happy result, although her writing flourishes in longer forms too, as in The Unfairy Tale and Before Dawn.

Janet Smith

Contents

Poppies

Ivan! Ivan! Get up! Screaming sirens mute Paula's shouts.

Some time back, jarring gunshot sounds had broken the sky's vast tranquillity, just as the mother and son were crossing the street to buy groceries.

The grocery shop window shatters into countless splinters, shards lodge in her son's leg like jigsaw pieces clicking into vacant slots, wounding him. The blood oozing out suggests he's been hit in the firing as well.

She sits there, with his head in her lap, trying to see if he is breathing, hoping time would stop right there and then and allow him to breathe forever.

A cesspit of red gathers around his body, confirming he has been shot.

Her legs go numb. She's too busy attending to him to notice that she's been shot as well, her own blood adding to the pool on the roadside.

From behind the shop window, a mournful face watches—too transfixed to act.

Paula keeps screaming and wailing. Ivan slumps into

unconsciousness, unable to withstand the trauma.

She tries to lift his limp body, but collapses along with it, producing a loud thud noise.

Blinking through misty eyes, helpless, she glances at the broken glass of the window, and the glass suddenly has a million red poppies on it. So many of them, swaying in the breeze.

She blinks again. The poppies are still there.

She is back in the poppy fields with him like they'd been last summer. Ivan had been laughing hysterically and taking pictures. It seemed like fables she recounted to him every night in bed.

Once upon a time, there lived a boy named Ivan in a town called Kyiv—who spent his summer vacations with his parents taking photos, imagining and dreaming of becoming a photographer one day.

Ivan's head is crouched in her lap, just as he has done so often before that, listening to his favourite lullabies. Paula holds him close to her bosom.

As he lies there soaked in blood, she looks at him and smiles. She wants to rewind the clock. Nobody can.

She hugs him and begins to hum a lullaby. She swings her head to and fro to see if help is coming, but the streets wear a desolate pallid look. The man in the grocery shop window is standing still, like a mannequin on display.

Last year, on his eighth birthday, Ivan's father had promised to take him again to the poppy fields on his ninth birthday. It's his birthday next week.

Wake up, Ivan, she implores. We'll go abroad. I'll take you to photograph poppies, just as papa promised. He'll be here soon.

Wake up, love. We have to plan your life, your birthday.

His silence hurts. She wants him to wake up and say *Mama I'm hurting; please take away my pain.*

But he does not complain. There is only one sound. Of silence.

Except for the booming battery of gunshots that stifle every other sound. Where are the birds? Their chirping seems remote, fading into non-existence. They've flown away in surprising synchronicity to find a safe refuge, where deafening alien sounds won't threaten their survival.

Her husband and she'd wanted to flee when the Russians attacked. Ivan's life is not the price she wants to pay for their decision to stick it out. *We should have run away like others to someplace safe...*

Thoughts trail off into emptiness from where all comes and to where all returns.

His silence doesn't hurt now. It scoffs. At the futility of the human race which in its infancy builds with blocks and toy stacks, but before long, in prodigal adolescence, gets bored of its own invented games and destroys what it built in a vacuous show of strength.

His silence slowly takes the shape of a barbed wire fence that separates me from you, this from that, them from us; dead from alive.

One more gunshot. A final sound fills the emptiness. She looks up at the window.

The millions of poppies on the window disintegrate into a large splatter of dark crimson blood that blotches its screen.

The Colour Of Water

1964. Civil Rights Act is in force. Courage is not.

Desegregation is permeating lexicons.

At the water fountains, worn-out wooden plaques read WHITES and COLOURED. Once polished to a high finish, they are useless now, hanging slackly, edges ragged - woeful cues that history changes but never erases.

Sally hesitates as she approaches them, her nerves defying time's playful trot.

In the wall mirror, her reflection appears darker, her lips cracked. She swallows saliva to wet her parched throat.

From beneath the COLOURED sign, water spouts. She takes a gulp, convinced that her colour is more than just a skin tone.

A New Dawn

"Good mahnin' darlin'" Karl addressed his tall frame in the full-length Victorian mirror. Self-love does not depend on someone else's approval.

It was an unusual day. Abraham Lincoln, the emancipator who would change history, had been elected president of America. Abolitionists tasted sweet victory, seeing a ray of hope at the end of a bitter struggle.

A lone cloud do carry its share ov silver linins', Karl thought, donning his leotard.

I have tah walk at 50 feet height today in dis col' weather. Life ov a travellin' acrobat ain't no easy.

Karl was born in America. As a boy, he helped his father, a free Black, rescue slaves from cruel owners. His father's abrupt disappearance left him devastated.

Two winters ago, he arrived in England for his debut tightrope show across the River Thames. After regaling the audience, he took his act to Hull. Soon after, he married Daphne, an Englishwoman, and settled in East Yorkshire, bidding farewell to a tumultuous past.

Bracing his shoulders, Karl strode across the rope suspended between two poles. He was blindfolded, chained, and pushing a wheelbarrow. To his brothers back home, this rare feat would symbolise triumph over oppression and injustice.

His bodysuit was soaked in sweat. Raucous hip-hip-hurrahs filled the air. Stagecoaches halted to watch.

The applause grew louder, as he reached the finish line. He released the cart, removed the blindfold, and squinted at the squealing crowd. Looking up, he noticed the sun dancing beneath the clouds, heralding a new dawn.

Moonlight Sonata

She'd been afraid of the tamarind tree outside, believing ghosts lived in its bark.

Not anymore.

She takes off a dangly earring, dons a diamond one to illuminate her jaded gown. The train hoots. Her hair stands. There's no railway track nearby. Since that train accident a week before her wedding, train whistles haunt her.

The night's cold, unforgiving. Dogs bawl.

Dressed in a white tuxedo, he's waiting by the tree. Her shadow emerges, earlobes flashing.

They rush to embrace. The wind strums Beethoven. They sway. As it crescendos, they unite, before suddenly vanishing.

Dogs stop the chorus. Leaves rustle.

Noor

It is a dark, cloudy, gloomy day in December, and most of the hilltops are blanketed in snow that surrounds the mountain ranges in a divine aura.

As Noor lies coated in slush and mud several hundred feet below, nature unleashes more fury, battering his face with icy cold pelts. In his final reckoning, buried beneath the regurgitating earth, he smiles, his lips pink from the cold but his thoughts warm with memories of Asma's head next to his on the pillow, urging him to marry her.

Life is a weft thread on a yarn that criss-crosses over the warps and is carefully laid out as per the rules. But every now and again, a thread with a distinct hue emerges from the fabric and refuses to blend in, smug in its oddity.

Noor runs a small clothing business in Kuber, a remote little hill village at the foot of the Himalayas. He never married and has no children of his own. After his brother's death, he's come to live with his brother's children and has taken over as the head of the family. He is a textile graduate who chose to settle in his hometown, turning down lucrative city offers. Kuber features high on tourist itineraries, so he gets a fair amount of business from them.

He spends hours with weavers, who consult him for his expertise, to design exquisite collections of weaves that sell like hotcakes during busy seasons. His shop's popularity has travelled far and wide and most tourists to Kuber stop by his shop to buy souvenirs.

This morning, as he gets ready to leave for the shop, black clouds and deafening thunder greet him; pearly raindrops mumble a melancholy recital, portending the arrival of something more dangerous. He's been uneasy all night, thinking about Asma—whom he hasn't seen since college—and their unfulfilled dreams.

The bleak morning sees him rescue his wet cat from scavenger hyenas lurking in the nearby bushes. He keeps her indoors for fear they will return for her. Perched on his favourite bar stool, he then demolishes his brunch and fingers the teacup in his hand for a few languid moments, wondering whether the Asma in Mumbai to whom he is sending today's order is actually *his* Asma.

Their house is an ancestral one, 150 years old and in need of repair. Once the weather calms down, he plans to renovate it. Many of the neighbours' houses had collapsed like a deck of cards in the storm the year before. But that storm was mild compared to what was expected now.

The humid air has left a mossy odour in the house. As the radio flickers on, the weather forecast warns that their town would see one of the worst storms. The town is on high alert, as mountains could heave a sigh any moment now. The children plead with him not to go outside, but he must since he needs to ship an *important* order to Mumbai right away—to Asma, who claims to be a great fan of his shop.

Mumbai may be home to many Asmas, but a strong hunch tells him this request is from his unrequited lady love from college, who had moved and married a businessman, brusquely truncating their love story midway.

Noor has never let go of their relationship. He yearns for her, staying awake at night hoping for a miracle, feeling generous in forgiving her for marrying someone else.

He sees her choice of someone else as a deception but hasn't let it cast a shadow over his love in all these years. On some days, he can see her face everywhere—in the bathroom mirror, the teapot, and even the weaving machines. But as soon as he moves closer to touch her, her lips pout in sarcasm before her face vanishes into thin air with the breeze.

The rain snarls louder, breaking into his thoughts. It's almost noon and Noor gets up to leave for the shop, notwithstanding the weather warning. He mounts his bicycle and pedals off, rolling down the hill. Raindrops pelt faster and harsher. He's wrapped in woollens from head to toe, with only his limbs and face exposed to the cold. It's not a good day for outdoors, but he needs to send *the* order. He'll hide a note for her under the scarves in the package. If Asma turns out to be his college love, it may rekindle old feelings.

Halfway through the ride, deafening thunder makes him halt and look back. As he looks up, the hill starts to crumble in front of him, and he watches wide-eyed, paralysed as a massive boulder heads in his direction.

And Winter Came

Jenny broke every patient-care rule. She dated John, who was in her care at the *Safe Home Wellness Retreat,* a rehabilitation centre for suicidal patients.

John suffered from chronic depression and attempted suicide. His psychiatrist had suggested this rehab facility.

Jenny, a senior caregiver there, initially called her feelings infatuation. But their growing chemistry made her scheme like never before.

Their momentous first meeting was at the reception. He was meticulously drilling a hole in his wrist with a pen he'd borrowed from the receptionist.

Jenny reacted sharply, "What're you doing, Mr…er…?"

His expression changed from blank to deep perusal, as if his temporal lobe was slow at processing information. Jenny enjoyed challenges.

He stood up to reveal a tall, broad-shouldered and attractive frame.

She recoiled as he raised his hand, expecting to be hit. But he quickly returned the pen.

Jenny, relax.

"Call me John." His smile could disarm an army battalion. "I'm not a fan of last names."

Jenny rolled her eyes. *The retreat is in for excitement.* She didn't realise she'd be feeding most of it.

She showed him around his room. He picked a glass vase from the television shelf and she snatched it.

"I shouldn't have left this here." *Paranoia? No! He's attempted suicide twice!*

"You're paranoid, ma'am. I'm only considering putting flowers in it."

Mind-reader? She thought nervously.

Jenny didn't expect them to converse much but he'd inspire her internal monologues.

She searched for any other potential *weapons* before leaving the room.

"You may call me Jenny," she yelled a parting shot, her cheeks turning bright pink.

*

The next few days were a blur of events, from getting-to-know-the-new-patient to falling-in-love. Awkward stares, blushing, stammering, attraction conspired to create dreamy moments.

That she could get fired for it didn't stop her.

She once overheard him fervidly deny something on the phone. "No, Emily, I swear I didn't. Trust me," he pleaded. "It's dad's and to be disposed of as instructed."

Jenny's mind invented possibilities. *His depression was caused by a failed relationship. Emily is his ex-wife who wants their house in alimony.*

Before long, she had a late-night visitor.

"I've come to see John." The girl was in her twenties, tall as him, dark-haired, and strikingly pretty.

Jenny's heart lunged.

"You can't. Visiting hours are over." She lied.

"It's important." The voice was urgent.

Really? Jenny pondered. *How pushy! You're why he's in rehab.*

"Are you Emily?"

"Yes, of course. Has he mentioned me?"

"No! He's taking treatment. I'm a caregiver. We have *no* personal conversations." *Another lie!*

"We're closing up."

The woman looked distressed. "He's not taking calls. I must see him."

Jenny was unfazed. "He needs rest. If he doesn't answer calls, we can't force him to."

She waited until the woman left. Then dashed upstairs to don a shimmering bodycon with a low back and a navel cut. Her fingers brushed over her belly button and she improvised her moves for their first date.

*

She slept in his room after that. She'd return to hers before dawn, slip into a staider nightdress and feign sleep. Tongues wagged easily around the retreat's community. She didn't want to be seen as exploiting a mentally fragile person.

Her strange behaviour went unnoticed. She'd never been happier. The centre became her dating venue, home, workplace rolled into one—utterly self-sufficient.

Each time she flouted regulation, she told herself manipulative women were more successful than idealistic ones who'd only ever make it to awards lists.

Emily returned five times. Jenny always had an excuse.

"He doesn't want to see you."

"He's resting as he had a bad night."

"Please don't come without calling."

"I relayed your message, but he refuses to meet you."

"You're wasting your time and mine."

The last of the excuses was slightly more accurate though.

Emily stopped coming. Jenny continued dating. John's health improved.

Gossip started circulating faster than a hunting cheetah. Hushed sniggers greeted her and she swallowed insults with exemplary fortitude.

*

Another midriff-baring dress. She admired herself in the mirror.

Turn him into a devoted puppy who only purrs on seeing his owner.

She'd quelled all qualms about toying with the feelings of a man who relied on her for support.

Her belly button was exposed, and it held a mini-Armageddon-like whirlpool that drew her into a vortex of conflicting emotions.

I won't let Emily sabotage this story.

*

Each night, they ate by candlelight. Since caregivers weren't allowed outings with patients, their dates were confined to his room.

She secretly checked his phone lists; there were no Emily-related calls.

In formal conversations that went on record, John admitted he wasn't suicidal anymore but upset about a property matter. She didn't mention Emily or her visits.

In Jenny's narrative, Emily was a villain who coveted John's property and drove him to suicide and *she* was protecting him.

While organising his cabinet one evening, she discovered a gold band. Her brain spun, the room swirled, and the floor beneath collapsed.

Is this Emily's? Or for me?

She didn't ask, lest her make-believe world should shatter.

And so the summer ended…

*

…and winter came.

Jenny bought John a cashmere sweater on his birthday.

When she returned from shopping, the receptionist informed her that John had a lady visitor, but as Jenny had instructed, she wasn't allowed in.

Good.

"However, we got her to fill the visitor form. Here," She held it out.

Emily Bennett was the name on the form.

She didn't know John's surname. *Let's see what she calls herself—wife or ex-wife.*

A tenacious finger scrolled down to the 'relation to patient' field.

"Sister?" She whimpered.

"Sister!" She shrieked.

"What's wrong, Jenny?"

She slumped into a chair and requested a glass of water. Realisation sank in like a cracking seed being pulled deeper into the soil by its emerging roots.

I kept his sister from seeing him. All the dresses I invested in, the seduction, the travesty. The betrayal!

Her mind cartwheeled ideas, solutions. *Come out clean. Confess.*

On The Other Side Of The Comfort Zone

"Aren't you excited?"

"No, not particularly."

"But a little bit at least?"

"Happiness comes at a premium."

"You were so broken when your film flopped; you thought your reputation as a filmmaker was permanently injured. You had no takers. And look, now they are all back!"

"Because you glued me back together."

"You have an offer that is every filmmaker's dream. It's time to celebrate!"

"Your eyes were beautiful lakes that reflected the warm glow of the morning sun, inviting me to dream through them...your smile lit up your face like the defining flicker of a sole candle in an unlit room."

"C'mon, cheer up. You're missing the woods for the trees. This is your comeback—your chance to show them what you can do. You are *not* a has-been."

"The balm you anointed my bruises with helped me through my worst days. And this new film plot—it was your idea, of course. It came from you. Our relation...was an unequal mathematical equation where I could never match your generosity."

"I can picture your award night already where you are winning back the honours. We are sitting in the front row, dressed in our best, and when your thank you speech mentions me, I beam with pride."

"You were always happy giving, giving, giving and I was only taking, taking, taking. We built ourselves a strange comfort zone in an unequal equation with the scale tilting on one side, and we didn't want to leave that zone, no matter what. We didn't want to tilt the scale back. Which part of you did the magnanimity come from? Try as I might, I could never find it in me."

"And then at the gala dinner after the award ceremony, you would go down on your knees and propose to me."

"This used to happen so often, didn't it? We had conversations without really having them because you were saying something totally disjointed from what I was speaking of. You were blinded by the dreams and I was deaf to them...and you. I was an oaf, never really seeing you for the beautiful woman you were, just seeing you as a means to fulfil my desires. I'm so sorry."

"Then afterwards, to celebrate, we can go on that long-planned Caribbean cruise that we've been talking of forever."

"That little dream on the edge of a cruise to nowhere stood there for as long as ever. Until *ever* was shortened to *now*, and *now* became *never.*"

"Hush! Believe in it, honey. Dream the way I do—in small instalments that add up to big things."

"For years, darling, I didn't do anything for you except take, take, take. I feel rotten for the way I treated you...used you."

"Get back home so I can make your favourite dinner and you can start working on the script and planning."

"You remember the rough sea we faced on a yacht before my film flopped? I was ready to abandon the ship and you...and what did you do? You asked them to save me first! This is what I mean...I was thinking of myself only and you were thinking of me only."

"I am going to design your clothes for your big night."

"Your eyes held stars in them; celestial bodies radiating so much positive energy that when it reached me, it swooped me off my feet and sprinkled a lot of it on me and made me believe."

"Let's pick up your favourite hot chocolate and marshmallows from Starbucks on the way home; tonight, we'll have a small treat."

"You knitted woollens for our baby who was to come but couldn't make it into this world because of my selfish decisions. I'm sorry. It was all me, me, me. And never you, you, you. Give me a chance to atone, will you? I will change everything. I'll be a new, new, new man."

"I like you just the way you are; my hero."

"You were blind to my flaws, my insensitivity."

"I think I have my Mr Perfect in you."

"I wish I could have saved you. I wish I'd tilted the scale back. I wish I'd married you as that's what you always wanted...that's what you *only* wanted."

"I don't want to die. I want to be on that cruise with you; on your award night when you thank me, the gala dinner you propose to me at; in that maternity ward delivering our baby; I want to be there before I die."

"The doctor said you didn't have long and I wanted to give you everything before we parted."

"I want you to bring me only flowers tonight; mind you, *only* flowers."

"I've got you flowers; here, your favourite pink roses. I hope they keep you warm as you sleep under this unyielding frosty earth, with your dreams...and mine."

The Unfairy Tale

Such mornings tend to be obscure and dull, like a blank slate ready to be scribbled on with chalk. Mornings that no one wants to wake up to. Even the bright lights from cars parked outside the castle weren't enough to lift the smoggy despair that crept in unannounced through the grey sky with the first rays of light.

Sirens blared, unsettling the morning's eerie silence. Inside, the bloodless body of a princess lay at the bottom of the stairs, her heartbeat frozen in a cold jerky moment.

As word of the tragedy spread, ambulances, police vans, and fire engines flocked outside the royal walls like bees around dandelions sniffing for nectar in the details. The drizzle from the sky mingled with the tears gently surging in the eyes of many of the royal staff members. She wasn't the most popular princess but wasn't the most hated either. Gossip that morning was hotter than the coffee being served, with much speculation on whether it was an accident or a murder.

Police collected forensic evidence to investigate the cause of death. Stuart was seen sitting motionless near the dead princess, his unslept eyes fixed on a spot near the body, his catatonic face contorted with just a hint of grief. He couldn't bear to look at her dead body and kept staring at that spot for so long as if eternity was on an indefinite house arrest on this bleak morning.

Sooner or later, they'd summon him for questioning; all he told them so far was that he had no idea what time she left their room last night and fell down the stairs or passed out; he never heard a wail or a sound, nor a scream or cry for help. He skipped some details about the evening—the passion that he could vividly view through his mind's lens.

She was sprawled at the final stair like a tattered doll with broken limbs and his thoughts kept returning to the previous night's lovemaking; her body enticing, his stress dissipating as he bent down to stroke her.

The staff gave him sorry looks. It was difficult for him to reconcile the incredible pleasure he felt last night with the revulsion he felt now, looking at her dead torso draped in a see- through gown sprangled unceremoniously on the floor.

He stared at a space somewhere near her head at first, then at the stag head so enchantingly mounted on the wall, all the time thinking about how alive she was the night before—alive, warm, and melting—and how dead she was now—dead, cold, and stiff.

Edward, her adopted son, phoned the butler, but was speechless; he tried speaking but barely managed to sniffle, his words and voice failing him. He was waiting for his charter flight to bring him back to his mother for a last look. As he sat there deep breathing to try and relax, thoughts of Stuart fed his lungs more than the air he inhaled, infuriating him that there was a possibility of his complicity in her death in some way. He had never approved of him, or any of his mother's other choices. He was ready to believe this was a planned murder.

The princess was a nonconformist, flouted every royal protocol, never married, and adopted a boy, who had been orphaned after a close friend died in an air crash at the young age of 20—much to the displeasure of her queen grandmother.

Edward was barely three years old when his adoptive single mother brought him to the castle. As he waited now at the airport's special wing, he recollected his time with her as a child, their vacations, and his first day at school, which became a mega-event as a royal family member was choosing to drive down herself to drop her son off. His matriculation, his school farewell – the princess did not miss a single important milestone of his life.

Mottled recollections become hazy with time, almost like his teary-eyed vision of the aerodrome from the waiting lounge right now. Some memories had gone missing, which the old family albums could help piece together.

He never cared for rumours that arose out of the fact that she was nearly 40 and still single. *What if she couldn't be the best contender for a queen?* She was the best mother in the world for him.

For Edward, Stuart was the wrong choice from day one. He was a wealthy businessman, but a philanderer on the verge of losing his fortune – or so the rumour in London's financial circles went. He met the princess at a ball and immediately activated his charm button to woo her. Though she wasn't fooled by his flattery, by the next day, he had moved in with her into the royal castle – in yet another breach of decorum.

Edward was not privy to details of her affair, as she kept them a secret, wanting to protect him from the vexatious paparazzi and turgid rumours. He would be the next king because the family had no other heirs. She wanted for him a *real* fairy tale life, unlike what she herself had.

Now and then after Stuart's entry into her life and the royal abode, press hounds would wait at the long-walled palace gates each morning, jumping up and down as if on an invisible trampoline, for a sight of the not-so-royal pair—as they dubbed them—and secretly tried to record them on cameras.

Two mornings earlier, Edward received a call from his mother, whose voice started with a heavy sob that tapered off after many long seconds, before she started to speak again; she said she was missing him. But this was so unlike her. She would never cry if she missed him. She would just hop on to the next flight and go over to meet him. He pressed her to tell him what was bothering her, in an unobtrusive sort of way, but his sustained enquiry made her uncomfortable and anxious, and she quickly hung up saying she would prefer to speak to him in person than over the phone.

They were due to meet at a painting exhibition in Paris the next week. Often, when they needed to discuss something important, they would pretend to enlist for an event and find a spot abroad, away from the ubiquitous CCTV cameras, to discuss important matters. Since he was a child, this had been their modus operandi.

He knew his mother had enemies for she had rubbed many the wrong way, but would anyone go to such lengths? Kill her? Or did she actually slip and fall? Or worse still, a suicide? The last he spoke with her, she had been sobbing uncontrollably.

Before that day, he had never heard such cavernous grief in her voice, which sent ripples of hollow echoes through the air around her. His mother was the rock on which his entire universe was built; he had many fans, friends, and followers at a young age, but they were just embellishments on a foundation *she* gave him. For him, this loss was irreparable.

Ten days after the body was found at the final stair, the police found nothing and got nowhere. They were now questioning only for sake of it, in the full knowledge that the fall was nothing more than an accident. It wasn't a suicide, murder, or conspiracy. It was plain stupidity perhaps – but the police hesitated to say it – that she was walking out of her room to go into the next in a sheer negligee and a seven-and-half-inch pointed heels. Stuart claimed he heard her humming as she left the room and then fell asleep. She was partly drunk and didn't watch her step. The police found a broken shoe heel, which had a secret compartment but there was nothing in it. It was empty.

The degree of sympathy a public figure gets is proportional to the number of scandals from which they emerge unscathed. In the case of the princess, it would be very hard to garner such support because of her blotchy past and failed affairs. So, along with her mortal remains, public sympathy was buried beneath the dirt, albeit over a week, with the scale ranging from "very sympathetic" on the first day to "life continues" on the seventh.

What would have been otherwise an open-and-shut case for the police became slightly protracted for the sake of formalities they had to go through since they were dealing with the *mysterious* death of a royal family member.

Edward told them about that strange phone call she had made two days before her death, trying to hold back her sobs in a totally uncharacteristic way, as if hiding something important that was upsetting her. But this wasn't enough of a hunch for the police to investigate.

Edward knew that his mother kept a secret diary, the whereabouts of which he was not aware. He also knew she hid pieces of paper in her sandals, which her designer specially fabricated for this purpose. But the police found no dead giveaways in her sandal heels. If she was hiding something, it's gone with her now, forever.

Their family physicians and psychiatrists told them she was on sleeping pills and it was not entirely inconceivable that she had taken them with alcohol that night, making her more drunk than usual. They didn't think that was the reason for her fall, though.

Many authors approached Edward about writing her biography posthumously but he shied from agreeing to it or revealing any unpleasant details. People knew her life was not a rose- scented Cinderella narrative. She didn't scam her way to any midnight balls and find her prince charming nor had she any fairy godmothers for allies. All she had was a string of unpleasant lovers who had put her off marriage at an early age, and she had no reason—in the form of a lover or otherwise—to change her mind after that.

Stuart lost his privilege to stay in the royal dwelling, which was one of the first things Edward ensured when he was formally recognised as the future king. Since he was almost broke at the time, Edward agreed to pay him some money until he could recover his bearings, and he did this to honour his mother's memory, not out of compassion for a man he despised but had made peace with.

With the secrets of the diary and the heels lost forever, Edward had no reason to believe Stuart tried to kill her. The lack of any motive was another reason he was forced to give him a clean chit.

On Stuart's last day in the castle, as they went through the garden skywalk straddling the two towers near the entrance, Edward surprised him by suddenly looking him straight in the eye and asking, "You killed her, didn't you?"

Much to his dismay, Stuart replied calmly, but firmly. "Edward, I know you don't like me and won't believe it, but I was growing fond of your mother and had begun to love her in a way I had never experienced love before, as trite as that might sound."

Edward looked hard at him for any facial signs of deception, but he could sense the honesty in his eyes and speech. He had truly started liking her.

Then, slightly embarrassed by the way he confronted him, his tone turned soft, laced with nostalgia, "It is tough for anyone who knows my mother to dislike her. She was a wonderful lady, and I don't say that only because she was my mother."

Stuart smiled, "She was wonderful, yes. I'm not saying this because she was my partner. Or a princess."

Edward smiled back as if to make amends since there was little else they agreed on. Then he turned around and walked a few steps, straight into a battery of reporters and photographers flashing mikes and bulbs in his face, and he immediately realised he had to brace himself for a new life, one that his mother had been preparing him for. A life she had gifted him—*a fairy tale*.

Before Dawn

She wakes up to the ebb and tide of waves washing over her on a seashore of memories. Sunlight thrusts in through the thick drapes, and a whiff of air brings in the aroma of tea that fires up her nostrils, transporting her back to a childhood spent in a cultured Victorian house.

Evocative smells make her senses more alive. Days are not

productive, just wondrous oblivion.

She stares at the alien blue walls. The white linen is blinding; an odometer is clipped on her finger, an IV needle is stabbed into her wrist, and a tiny bit of blood has spilled out on the bedsheet as if an artist has just started to dribble red paint on a blank canvas. She shuts her eyes trying to recall; memory flashes leave her hot.

"There's a medical emergency...a car accident...we suspect multiple fractures."

She opens her eyes. The blue walls look familiar. How long has it been? Days? Weeks? Months? The beeping monitor indicates she's alive, not dreaming or hallucinating, confirming her heart is beating, though she knows it used to beat for better reasons.

A man walks in, dressed in the same shade as the walls. She tries to recognise him but he is as strange as the surroundings.

"Ma'am, how're you this morning? Do you remember anything at all now?"

Has he asked this before? She tries hard to form a sensible thought, but words fail her. She can neither recall her name nor who she is.

She allows the bubbles in her sparkling wine to settle before sipping it. Tonight is the celebration. She'd be free, forever. It's her fifth drink; she needs the intoxication to do what she is daring to.

In the bar cabinet's mirror, she catches a glimpse of her husband's frail body, slouched cosily in his wheelchair. He is on the other side of the room, sipping his tea, with the help of the male nurse attending to him. She gestures to the man to leave, before starting to move in the direction of the wheelchair.

They hear the attendant close the heavy mahogany front door. They're both alone now. She gazes at his body, with a disgusted expression. He's been paralysed for many years and is little more than a vegetable in a wheelchair who needs nurses and doctors to keep him alive.

But you won't make it through this evening, she gives him a crooked smile. He looks terrified as he stares at her, as though he knows she's plotting something sinister and he'll be taken to a slaughterhouse. They don't exchange dialogue with their eyes. His eyes are petrified, while hers are icy.

She walks toward him in her inebriated state, grabs his wheelchair and starts racing it toward the balcony. He's lost his ability to speak due to paralysis. He tries to make muffled sounds, but she laughs out loud because she knows no one can hear him. She wheels him into the balcony through the glass door, his heart jogging.

She stands in front of him, gently touches his face, and then scoops him in her arms. He knows this is the end and pleads with his eyes. She observes that he has a similar expression to her dog's when he was sick and about to die. As she inches closer to the edge, his eyes expand more in their sockets, anticipating what will come next.

She pays no heed to his eyes. Without wasting time, she swings his body like a discus and flings him off the balcony railing of their 20th-floor penthouse apartment. It swims in the air for a brief fraction of a microsecond before being sucked in by gravity.

It is over. She is free to marry the man she loves, free from being tied to an invalid husband who is no more than a lifeless body with no feelings.

She comes back inside, with no signs of regret. Before anyone discovers his body, she must flee. They'll ask questions as to how a man who's unable to stand up from his wheelchair without assistance falls off the balcony.

She grabs the car keys and rams the front door after her. Slamming the car out of the garage, she speeds out into the pitch-black night.

She's excited. She'll see *her lover* and inform *him* that they can finally get married. As she speeds on the motorway, she doesn't notice the large cargo truck in front of her.

She hits her foot on the brakes but it's too late. Her car crashes into it. Blackness.

When she wakes up, she is in a room with unfamiliar blue walls, with no memory of who she is or how she got there.

Sara had stormed out of her house a few weeks ago in a huff after arguing with her stepmother who'd stolen her fiancé and was planning to marry him.

She wasn't sure whether to feel sorry for her father who's been strapped to a wheelchair for years now, or herself, since she was losing her man to her stepmother, who'd been deceiving both her father and her.

Since she was not prepared to deal with this situation, and the only man who could advise her was in no position to, she left the apartment and moved out on her own.

Tonight, two bone-chilling phone calls leave her speechless.

The first is from a neighbour informing her that her father's body has been discovered in the building's front yard; he has fallen from the 20th-floor balcony and died.

She's shocked.

Her father was the only ray of hope in this bleak life after she learnt of her stepmother and fiancé's affair. She visited him frequently, just to reinforce the fighting spirit she needed to survive on her own.

The second phone call is from the police, informing her that her mother has been in an accident on the highway and has been taken to the hospital, and the family needs to come and take care of the paperwork.

Family? Sara ponders. She stole my fiancé from me. She was leaving my father to wed my fiancé.

She knows what she has to do. She leaves for her father's house for he is more important to her than the woman lying in the hospital they are asking her to help.

Her sobs are interspersed with hiccups all the way to his house. The neighbours have pieced his body together and placed him on the bed, waiting for Sara.

He couldn't even stand up himself, how did he fall off the balcony? The thought niggles at the back of her mind but something else that needs her attention takes precedence.

On seeing him, she perches a kiss on his forehead. *He deserved better.* She starts making arrangements for his funeral.

Her next stop that night is the hospital that has been calling her repeatedly. As she is completing the formalities at the reception, she runs into the doctor who's taken her stepmother to the operation room.

"Ma'am, nothing can be said right now. She has suffered multiple fractures as well as a brain concussion. I'm surprised she's even alive. We are doing everything possible."

As Sara emerges from the hospital's front door, the strobe lights from the opposite building make her squint. Through moist eyes, she looks up at the starry sky. Her father's voice, which she hasn't heard in years, rings loud in the cold night air. When she'd lost her mother at the age of 15, in an attempt to console her, her father had said: *Sara, always remember, it's the darkest before dawn.*

The Dark Room

Annie furiously scribbled on her notepad.

Remorse is a dark room you enter only to develop the negatives of the photographs you shot on that great voyage through life where you inadvertently injured someone badly.

Regret is the chocolate you never ate, even though it was delicious and right in front of your eyes, within your budget, but you didn't buy it.

Guilt is like the troublesome insect you killed for constantly bothering you; once squatted, it can be squatted without hesitation again.

Annie's life was devoid of these emotions she jotted down in her notepad.

She felt no remorse for killing her husband in cold blood. She never regretted the decision to abandon her child. And guilt was a troublesome insect that she squashed every time it tried to spread its wings.

You need to forgive yourself, Annie. It's natural to feel vengeful when someone has hurt you and wronged you, her best friend and psychiatrist advised her.

Annie's relationship with her deceased husband was far from normal. Within two years of marriage, she realised it would never be normal, but she endured the abuse for five years, before poisoning his food.

Before quietly performing his last rites, with no attendance there as she didn't inform any of his family, she took the sharpest knife from the kitchen cabinet and stabbed him many times in the chest, killing a dead man even more. She stabbed his heart repeatedly until her entire gown was soaked in blood.

She left her child in an orphanage, as she felt no love for a child born of rape. As she walked away from the gate, she didn't turn around to see her daughter staring after her—lost and puzzled.

If she had surrendered, she could have made a case of self-defence and got exonerated by the courts and bought her freedom, but how would she be free from the odd stares of neighbours, which would remind her every day of the crime she committed, and even worse, the crime he committed behind closed doors every day for five years?

Her daughter had the same eyes as him. Annie couldn't bear to look at her without being reminded of him. How could she not think of him when she looked at her face? She felt the urge to slap the child thinking she was slapping him hard. What would people say if they saw her beating her child because she hated her eyes? They'd label her an atrocious mother, and her exoneration by the courts would have no bearing on the incarceration she'd face in their looks.

What she did was her only alternative.

She changed her name, her passport, and illegally lived under an assumed identity in a foreign country, where no one recognised her or asked her any questions. She had to evade the immigration authorities for some time but eventually they stopped hounding her.

She was a cleaner for two hours in the morning, a shop assistant for two hours in the afternoon, a librarian for an hour in the evening, and a self-proclaimed author for the rest of the night.

She was starting her first book and trying to frame its opening sentence.

Freedom is like a baby bird learning to open its wings to take the flight that will set its spirit free from the shackles that have bound it.

It was Annie's big award night. She was being awarded an honour for the contributions to literature in the country of her current residence. Her entire life's struggles were being acknowledged and compensated for at this award night.

She knew she would steal these moments away from the hours she spent brooding in the dark haloes of her imagination, afraid to come out into the light.

It had been 30 years since she left her country. But she could never escape the desolate past, which reared its ugly head in the dark themes of all her writings, refusing to go away. *Changing one's identity does not kill the demons usually.* She'd reconciled that she'd never find closure in this life.

She never looked back nor cared. It wasn't easy being on her own in a foreign land for she decided never to marry or have another relationship. All she did for 30 years was scribble away on her notepad, crystallizing the carbon of her mind to diamond, and here she was—sporting a tiara made of those diamonds. She was receiving one of the most prestigious awards for her literary talents.

The host of the evening blared her name into the microphone, breaking her reverie. She summoned the courage to rise up—as they put the spotlight on her—and walk onto the stage to collect the award from a promising writer from her native country, who had previously won the Young Writers Award.

As she reached closer to the podium, the writer holding her citation smiled at her. Annie looked at her and froze. She started turning pale, as the darkness grew darker. Before she fainted, she felt those familiar pair of eyes stab the centre of her heart and rip through to her soul.

Walking With Ghosts

The world can't bury September 11, for TV screens and newspapers have a way of resurrecting the phantoms.

Time's been in a deep freeze since the towers were crushed like graham crackers for a cheesecake crust, resulting in an outcome nowhere as sweet as the dessert.

Governments condemned; military forces boiled—the stage was set for a retaliation. Rhetoric of 'freedom in peril—innocents must be saved' raised its head every now and then.

Tortuous moulds sat festering on open wounds, not letting people become complacent and making it difficult for them to trust again.

A country at war causes unrest at home. Various subplots emerge from the main conflict— secret operations and denouements—and the world awaits a climax.

One man, far from Ground Zero, in another country, Britain, who lost his fiancé in the attacks, knew how to set things right. Not in his life, but in the planet's.

In his shadow lurked sorrow that followed him around until the sun set, only to give him back his companion the next morning.

On his hand, he wore the last of a promise, refusing to take it off, a diamond-inlaid ring that dazzled—its light exposing his void, pulling him into an emotional black hole.

Most labelled Harry as MI6's backbone. When MI5 bosses retired, they moved him to MI6; they almost never relieve their finest men. In six years of service, he'd worked in many countries—Iraq, Pakistan, Afghanistan, Russia, the UK and the US—and upset devious terrorist designs, averted tragedies.

As morning rays filtered through slits in curtains that rustled with the breeze, he sat by the phone, waiting for it to ring. Shortly, he was on a hotline to the White House in Washington, D.C.

The FBI had raided a terrorist funding suspect's house and found replicas of Westminster Palace along with blueprints in his child's room; the child had no use for them and they were more than vacation souvenirs. They made arrests and were questioning them, but no further progress had been made. Britain was alerted.

Two hours later, Harry boarded the Eurostar to Calais. As the train coursed through the dark tunnel at high speed, he started typing on his tablet. Nine years after the US attacks, an MI5 report showed the same terror group was planning an assault on London. Their leader, underground in a remote part of France, close to Paris, was receiving help from one of the MI6 agents.

Nine years. He looked at the diamond bulge parked on his finger like a painful sore, wondering if he will ever be alive again.

The Eurostar crossed the tunnel in 20 minutes—enough time for Harry to plan his *Hacksaw Mission.* He was travelling *Standard Premier*—over the years, he'd mastered courting luxury with the same finesse with which he courted danger. As breakfast came, he eyed it like a caged bird eyes his food, undecided. Nausea and déjà vu washed over him and he shut his eyes, hoping his lids would veil a lot more than his mood.

Paris was going to be a reincarnation of India. He was putting the traitor to sleep and there was a hacksaw in his briefcase, hungrily waiting for a lick.

A silent war causes more damage than an actual one—with enemies and weapons almost invisible—one that claims to be just.

Last year, on a secret operation in India, he went to meet his aide, knowing he'd find him dead there—*a part of the plan.* When he arrived on the third storey of the half-built structure, he found his throat slit by a hacksaw, his eyes bulging out of their sockets, his head cradled in a red puddle of blood trickling from his neck. Close to his torso lay the weapon, whose glinting metal with a thin red line smirked at him.

Harry didn't regret it afterwards; whatever guilt he felt was gone since his aide had turned the enemy's informer. He usually played by the rulebook, never hurting an ally, but sometimes, *small* sacrifices had to be made to win *big* wars, and secret service agents were no different than soldiers, when it came to martyring.

This time, he had to do it himself. *It's not going to be easy.* He wore black so the dark colour would supersede any mottled red stains.

He skipped the flight to Paris and took the train to dodge his assassins, who were waiting at the airport for him. He'd been on their radar for years and they were always either a step ahead of or behind him, but never far.

After having survived many attempts on his life—one he wilfully signed up for when he joined the secret service—he liked to keep them guessing. He brought his sister Sandra and her kids along to make it look like a family outing.

Outside the window, the dark tunnel wall raced at supersonic speed. *Inside, a dark wall of vengeance refused to dissipate, despite fissures starting to appear.*

Harry smiled looking at the kids, who were engrossed in their phones, oblivious to the role they were playing in this episode of their uncle's secret life.

It's easier to train a dog for espionage than exact loyalty from a man, he thought as the train turned within the tunnel on the journey's last leg. He dropped his head to snooze, having decided on his plan.

"Sir, care for a drink?" The host's shrill voice and grunting food trolley woke him up. He shoved him aside and rushed to the restroom, holding back the rising bile.

Ten minutes later, he emerged, wiping his mouth with the back of his hand, noticing they had left the tunnel behind.

As the train entered Paris, he waved a hand at the kids, taking a long moment to savour their smiles before pirouetting onto the platform. Glancing at familiar surroundings, his eyes settled on the neon-sign clock, and he released a sigh. *It's never easy.*

About the Author

Arunima Hoskote

Arunima Hoskote has spent most part of her life writing and editing for corporate clients. In more recent years, she has published a book of poetry called Ellipses and another book of short fiction called The Vantage Point. Having spent close to two decades in the writing industry, she is now focusing on developing her flash fiction. Her microfiction story, The Colour of Water, received fourth place in the 1st round of the prestigious NYC Midnight Challenge. Her stories have also been published in the Indian journal Muse India as well as a Singapore journal.